W9-BZH-385

# The
# DRAGON
# in
# the
# CLOCK
# BOX

# The DRAGON in the CLOCK BOX

By M. JEAN CRAIG

Illustrated by

Kelly Oechsli

W · W · NORTON & COMPANY · INC · New York

*For* MARTIN,
and because of him

On Tuesday afternoon Joshua's mother went shopping and bought a new alarm clock. When she unwrapped it, Joshua asked her if he might have the box it came in.

"Of course, Josh, if you like. What are you going to do with it?"

"Something," answered Joshua, but politely.

On Wednesday Joshua's mother saw that he had taken some paper tape and sealed the clock box closed again. Every slit and every corner was tightly covered. And wherever Joshua went and whatever he did, he kept the clock box with him.

When he played with his soldiers on the side porch,
he put the clock box on the porch step, in the sun.

When he ate supper, he set it under his chair.

When he went to bed, he laid it next to his pillow.

"Can you tell me what you have in the clock box?"
asked Joshua's mother, when she was tucking him in.

"Yes. I can."
"Well—what?"

"It's a dragon's egg," said Joshua.

"I see... Joshua–is it really?"

"Yes, it is. Really," said Joshua, and went to sleep.

On Thursday, at breakfast time, Joshua's father asked him, "How is your dragon's egg doing this morning, Josh?"

"It isn't *doing*. It's just waiting."

"What on earth is it waiting for?" asked Joshua's big sister.

"For it to be time," answered Joshua. "I would like some toast, please."

"Time to hatch, I suppose?" And Joshua's big sister giggled as she passed him the toast.

"Yes, time to hatch," said Joshua, without smiling even a little bit. "I would like some jam on it, please."

"I hear you have a dragon's egg in that box of yours," said Joshua's big brother when he came home from high school late in the afternoon. "How did it get there?"

"The mother dragon laid it there," said Joshua. "Before."

"Before? What do you mean, before? Before what?" asked Joshua's big brother.

"Before I sealed it up. Of course," Joshua answered him, and he picked up the clock box and went out of the room with it.

That evening Joshua's father wanted to know how any air could get into the box when it was taped shut.

"It doesn't need air yet," explained Joshua. "It just needs to be warm and quiet. Until it's hatched."

"When is it going to hatch?" asked Joshua's big brother.

"When it's ready to," Joshua told him.

"But how will you know when it's ready to?" Joshua's big sister asked him, not laughing this time.

Joshua looked at her for a minute before he spoke again.

"*I* don't have to know. *It* will know." And then in a whisper, to himself, he added, "Silly."

On Friday morning, Joshua came down to breakfast a little bit late. He put the clock box on the table close to his plate, instead of under his chair. There was a small, neat hole cut in one corner of it.

"He's a boy dragon," Joshua told his mother as he sat down.

"He hatched.

Last night.

Very late."

Joshua's mother spoke softly. "How can you tell?"

"It was time."

"Did you hear it?"

"*Him,* not *it.* No, he was very quiet. But it was time, and he was ready, so I knew. So I made a hole just now. Because now he needs air."

"And now you can peek through the hole to see what he's like," said Joshua's big sister.

"I know what he's like. He's like a baby dragon. Just hatched."

"But you could look, just to be sure, couldn't you?"

"I am sure," said Joshua. "And he doesn't want me to look yet. Because he's very young. He wants to be all alone for a while."

On Saturday, Joshua's mother and his father and his big sister and his big brother all happened to be rather busy all day. It wasn't until nearly bedtime that anyone spoke to him again about the clock box.

"Do you still have a baby dragon in that box, Josh?" his brother asked him.

"Yes," said Joshua.

"Have you seen him yet?"

"Yes," said Joshua. "Now I have."

"Say, that's wonderful! What does he look like?"

"He's pink, a little.

His wings are still soft.

With goldy edges I think.

Because it's dark in there."

"Then make the hole bigger, so you can see him better."

"No, I can't. He wants it dark. While his wings are so soft it has to be dark."

"How do you know that, Joshua?" his mother
asked him.

"It's always that way with dragons," said Joshua. "With baby boy dragons."

On Sunday morning, just before lunchtime, Joshua told his big sister, "His name is Emmeline."

1421933

"But Josh, that's a girl's name!"

"I know, but he's a Chinese dragon.

And Chinese boy dragons like

to have girls' names.

His eyes are purple.

And his wings are hardly soft at all now."

"May I see him?"

"No. He's too shy."

'But *you* look at him now, don't you?"

"He's used to me," said Joshua.

Monday evening Joshua's father asked him what he had been feeding the dragon.

"They don't eat when they're little," said Joshua. "Not baby dragons. Not while their wings are still even a little bit soft."

"Well, then, what are you going to feed him when his wings get strong?"

"I won't have to feed him then," answered Joshua,
and he laid his hand gently on the clock box.

And then it was Tuesday again, and Joshua came to the breakfast table without the clock box. But everyone was in a hurry to start the day, and no one noticed.

It was later, when Joshua's mother was making his bed, that she saw the clock box on the floor. The tape had been torn off and the box was open wide. It was empty.

"Joshua! Your dragon's gone!"

Joshua was busy taking his marbles out of a bag,
and he didn't turn around when he answered her.

"He was big enough last night.

And his wings were strong.

He flew away."

"Did he really? But, Josh, where could he fly to?"

Joshua turned around, then, and walked over to where the empty clock box was, and picked it up.

"Where dragons go," he said.

"This is a very good box to keep marbles in, I think.
I'm going to put my marbles in it now."

And he did.